No Longer Property Of
Washoe County Library

BOOKSTORE

RECEIVED
JUN 1 8 2016
NORTHWEST RENO LIBRARY
Reno, Nevada

D0577266

TO THE INTREPID GREAT MINDS OF BOOKS AND READING —D.M.

FOR MY MOTHER AND FOR ÉMILIE,
TO WHOM I OWE MANY A BORROWED BOOK... —J.B.

Text © 2013 Danielle Marcotte
Illustrations © 2013 Josée Bisaillon

English translation © 2016 Owlkids Books

Originally published as *Papa, maman, nos livres et moi*
by Les 400 coups

All rights reserved. No part of this publication may be reproduced,
stored in a retrieval system, or transmitted in any form or by
any means, without the prior written permission of Owlkids
Books Inc., or in the case of photocopying or other reprographic
copying, a license from the Canadian Copyright Licensing Agency
(Access Copyright). For an Access Copyright license, visit www.
accesscopyright.ca or call toll-free to 1-800-893-5777.

Owlkids Books acknowledges the financial support of the Canada
Council for the Arts, the Ontario Arts Council, the Government of
Canada through the Canada Book Fund (CBF) and the Government
of Ontario through the Ontario Media Development Corporation's
Book Initiative for our publishing activities.

Published in Canada by
Owlkids Books Inc.
10 Lower Spadina Avenue
Toronto, ON M5V 2Z2

Published in the United States by
Owlkids Books Inc.
1700 Fourth Street
Berkeley, CA 94710

Library and Archives Canada Cataloguing in Publication

Marcotte, Danielle [Papa, maman, nos livres et moi. English]
    Mom, dad, our books, and me / written by Danielle
Marcotte ; illustrated by Josée Bisaillon ; translated by Karen Li.

Translation of: Papa, maman, nos livres et moi.
ISBN 978-1-77147-201-2 (bound)

    I. Li, Karen, translator II. Bisaillon, Josée, 1982-, illustrator II.
Title. III. Title: Papa, maman, nos livres et moi. English.

PS8576.A6358P3513 2016   jC843'.54   C2015-906008-7

Library of Congress Control Number: 2015948455

Edited by: Jessica Burgess
Designed by: Barb Kelly

ONTARIO ARTS COUNCIL
CONSEIL DES ARTS DE L'ONTARIO
an Ontario government agency
un organisme du gouvernement de l'Ontario

Canada Council
for the Arts
Conseil des Arts
du Canada

Manufactured in Shenzhen, Guangdong, China, in November 2015,
by WKT Co. Ltd.
Job #15CB1195

A   B   C   D   E   F

Owl
kids Publisher of Chirp, chickaDEE and OWL
www.owlkidsbooks.com

Owlkids Books is a division of Bayard
CANADA

I love it when
we're all together:
Mom, Dad,
our books,
and me.

Mom reads. Dad reads.
And I read, too!

Buddy doesn't read.
He hasn't learned yet.

Toto doesn't read either.
He'd rather watch TV.

And forget Gracie.
She's much too busy.

But I'm not too busy.

I know how to turn pages,
name pictures, and
sound out words.

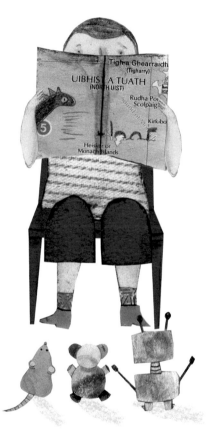

I can read now.
Like the big kids!

Everyone around me reads.
After five or six pages, Grandma's
head is in the clouds.

Grandpa takes cover beneath a canopy and sinks into his novel.

Uncle browses in a kitchen scented
with eggplants and thyme.

Auntie reads sheet music. She tells wonderful stories made of sound.

Pirate stories give my neighbor the shivers
as she swings safely in her hammock...

...while I like getting goose bumps
in my bubble bath.

And books are not the only things we read!

The fisherman reads the sky
for coming storms.

A woman reads love poems in her boyfriend's eyes.

A tourist reads the time
on his watch while checking
the train schedule.

Madam Dora reads the future
in tarot cards and crystal balls,
and in the lines of my palm.

Everyone in the doctor's office reads—from the nurses to the patients.

A baby chews on a board book while the doctor reads a thermometer.

Reading can
make you cry.

Reading can
make you smile.

I like it best
when I laugh *and* cry.

Thanks to books,
I find balance,
I climb high,
I follow new roads,
and I move forward.

But as far as books may take me,
I will never lose my way.
Because books also bring us together:
Mom, Dad, our friends, and me.